FOR MORE THAN A THOUSAND YEARS, the days from Christmas to the Epiphany (January 6—the day the three Magi offered the first Christmas gifts of gold, frankincense and myrrh) have been known as the Twelve Days of Christmas. Traditionally, they have been set aside for celebration, feasting, and gift giving.

The counting song in this book is the first carol known to celebrate this traditional gift-giving. It is said to date as far back as the 13th century, but it first appeared in print in England in 1780. The song became popular as a game played by children and adults. A player would start the game by reciting the lines of the song and then the group would repeat the lines, careful to keep the verses in order. Anyone who missed a line would have to give a gift to the group.

For my big-hearted In-Laws, Jacqui, Sandy, Laura Marie and
my wild and woolly Out-Laws, Sydney and Eric.

———

Illustrations © 1996 by Woodleigh Marx Hubbard. All rights reserved.
Book design by Lucy Nielsen and Suellen Ehnebuske. Lettering by Lilly Lee. Printed in Hong Kong.
The illustrations in this book were rendered in gouache.

Library of Congress Information Available. ISBN: 0-8118-1264-2

Distributed in Canada by Raincoast Books, 8680 Cambie Street, Vancouver B.C. V6P 6M9
Distributed in Australia and New Zealand by CIS Cardigan Street, 245-249 Cardigan Street, Carlton 3053 Australia

10 9 8 7 6 5 4 3 2 1
Chronicle Books, 275 Fifth Street, San Francisco, California 94103

WOODLEIGH MARX HUBBARD'S

Twelve Days of Christmas

chronicle books

SAN FRANCISCO

On the first day of Christmas
my true love
sent to me

a Partridge in a pear tree

On the second day of Christmas

my true love sent to me

and a  ★

2 Turtledoves

On the third day of Christmas my true love sent to me

2 ★ and a ★

3 French Hens

On the fourth day of Christmas my true love sent to me

A Calling Birds

3 ★ 2 ★ and a ★

On the fifth day of Christmas
my true love sent to me

4 ★ 3 ★ 2 ★ and a ★

On the seventh day of christmas my true love sent to me

6 ⭐ 5 ⭐ 4 ⭐ 3 ⭐ 2 ⭐ and a

7 Swans a Swimming

8 Maids a Milking

On the ninth day of Christmas my true love sent to me

9 Drummers Drumming

On the tenth day of Christmas my true love sent to me

10 Pipers Piping

On the eleventh day of Christmas my
true love sent to me

11 Ladies Dancing

4 ★ 3 ★ 2 ★ and a ★

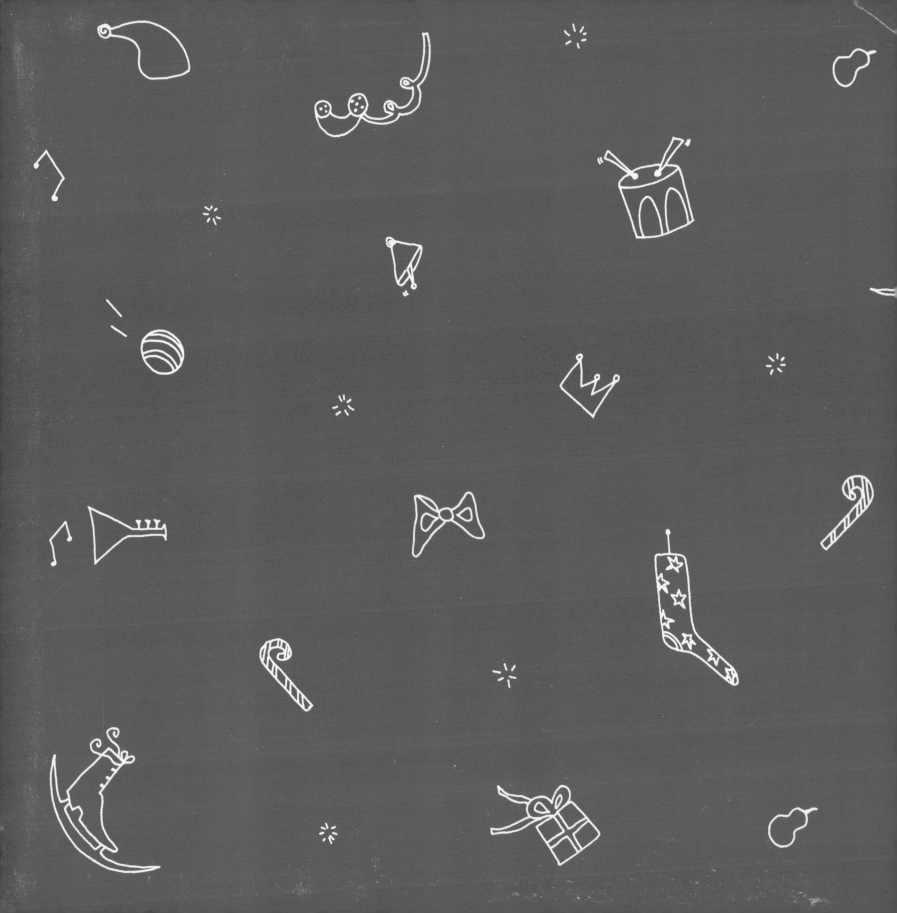